Edmund Gosse

Robert Browning

Personalia

Edmund Gosse

Robert Browning
Personalia

ISBN/EAN: 9783337142247

Printed in Europe, USA, Canada, Australia, Japan

Cover: Foto ©Andreas Hilbeck / pixelio.de

More available books at **www.hansebooks.com**

ROBERT BROWNING

Personalia

BY

EDMUND GOSSE

London
T. FISHER UNWIN
26 PATERNOSTER SQUARE
1890

The Riverside Press, Cambridge, Mass., U. S. A.
Printed by H. O. Houghton & Company.

PREFACE

IT would not have occurred to me that it was worth while to give a lasting form to the notes which are here reprinted. But I am assured by those who are peculiarly well fitted to know what is required by the readers of Browning that there is constant inquiry for the number of *The Century Magazine* (December, 1881) in which they appeared, and I am bound to confess that I am frequently written to by strangers who ask me to tell them where they can meet with the remarks in question. I have been, in consequence, requested by the poet's American publishers to allow the appended reprint to be made ; and the fact is that there is so

much of it which is Mr. Browning's, and
so little which is mine, that I have felt
it would be mock-modesty to refuse my
consent. "The Early Career of Robert Browning" was inspired and partly
dictated, was revised and was approved
of, by himself. It is here put forth,
with great diffidence, not as having any
final importance, but as a contribution
towards that biography of the great
poet which must one of these days be
written. The author of that life will,
I cannot but hope, turn to these pages
with some curiosity, and perhaps, until
his work is accomplished and this small
star buried in his sun, readers and lovers of Browning may be glad to see
what events in his early career seemed
notable to the poet himself. With this
modest purpose, and no other, I have
permitted these personal notes to be re-
deemed from the pages of an old magazine.

It has been suggested to me that I ought to explain the circumstances under which these data were collected. Ten years ago, it will be recollected, although Mr. Browning was recognized as a great poet, he had not yet excited that degree of personal curiosity which soon afterwards began to be awakened. The facts of his biography were put before the public in the most rudimentary form. The year of his birth was seldom given correctly; the month and day had, I think, never been made known. At that time I had the happiness of seeing him very frequently; for twelve years, I may perhaps mention, I was his close neighbor. I had several times ventured to point out to him how valuable would be some authentic account of his life, but he had always put the suggestion from him. I had ceased to hope that he would ever break through his reserve, when one morning in February, 1881, he sent round a note to me, saying, " Come ; and I will do what you wish." I went, and found him visibly annoyed by an account of his life, mainly fabulous, which the post had brought him. He said, " If you still wish to take down some notes of my life, I am willing to give you all the help I can ; I am tired of this tangle of facts and fancies." It was agreed that we should dedicate some hours in the morning, once a week, to this delightful task, and for about a month, at stated intervals, for a couple of hours at a time, I sat at his study table, while he perambulated, and I jotted rapidly down the notes of his conversation. At his suggestion, I came each morning provided with a schedule of questions, one of which I would read, and then let him weave the embroidery of his answer in whatever way he chose, until information languished, when I would put another question to him. At last I had collected a great mass of facts, gossip, and opinion, which I put into some rough order, and submitted to him. He marked for omission all that his maturer judgment did not wish to preserve. What was rejected was, much of it, of extreme interest, but he asked me to destroy it all, and of course I loyally did so. I then cast in literary form what he determined to let pass, and the article proceeded to America.

It appeared in the December number of *The Century Magazine*, and my little record would be incomplete if I did not publish, among my *pièces justificatives*, the note which Mr. Browning left at my door with his own hand, as soon as he had read the article in its published form : —

19 Warwick Crescent, W.
December 4, 1881.

My dear Gosse, — What am I to say,
or try to say? Your goodness and generosity there can be no doubt concerning; if
any reproach to your judgment happen on
account of all this partiality and praise,
your goodness and generosity must bear it
as well as they can. I wish yourself, when
the years come, may find such an apprecia-
tor. You will at least deserve such an one
— I hope and fear — better than does
Your affectionate Friend,
Robert Browning.

That this volume may make some
pretense to be a book, — lest, as Gray
said of his poems, "this work should be
mistaken for the works of a flea or a
pismire," — I have added to it some
slight recollections of the personal char-
acteristics of our illustrious friend, con-
tributed to *The New Review* for Janu-

ary, 1890. If such notes as these are to have any permanent value, they must be recorded before the imagination has had time to play tricks with the memory. Such as they are, I am sure they are faithful to-day ; to-morrow I should be sure of nothing.

EDMUND GOSSE.

March, 1890.

CONTENTS

THE EARLY CAREER OF
ROBERT BROWNING

THE EARLY CAREER OF ROB-
ERT BROWNING.

1812–1846.

IT is not my design in the following pages to attempt any exact review or any minute analysis of the writings of one of the most copious and versatile of modern poets. The range of Mr. Browning's genius is so wide, the temper of his muse so Shakesperean and universal, that he will probably exhaust the critical powers of a great many students of literature before he finally takes his right place among the chief authors of modern Europe. The constellation which is still ascending our poetical heavens is too much confused as yet by those mists of personal preju-

dice and meteors of temporary success
which always lurk about the horizon of
the Present to enable us to map the
stars in it with certainty. Many attempts, of course, have been made, and
some with a great measure of success.
Two such studies, among others, demand
recognition for their extent and author-
ity, — the volume on Mr. Browning's
poetry by Mr. John Nettleship, since
known as an animal-painter, and the
elaborate criticism printed in *The Century Magazine* by Mr. E. C. Stedman.
I shall not attempt to compete with
these or any similar reviews ; my purpose is to touch lightly on those early
volumes of Mr. Browning which are
comparatively less known to his admirers, and to enrich such bibliographical
notes as I have been able to put together
with a variety of personal anecdotes and
historical facts which now for the first

time see the light, and which I have jotted down, from time to time, from Mr.
Browning's lips, and with his entire consent and kindly coöperation. No one is
more alive than Mr. Browning, or, may
I add, than I, to the indelicacy of the
efforts now only too frequently made to
pry into the private affairs of a man of
genius, to peep over his shoulder as he
writes to his intimate friends, and to
follow him like a detective through the
incidents of a life which should not be
less sacred from curiosity than the life
of his butler or his baker. The poet
has expressed his mind with extreme
plainness :

"A peep through my window, if folks prefer ;
But, please you, no foot over threshold of mine."

But literary history, the most charm-
ing of all occupations of the human
mind, as Warburton said, is a very different thing from personal history, and

there are certain facts about the development of a poet's intellect and the direction that it took, the welcomes that it received and the reverses that it endured, about which curiosity is perfectly legitimate. For those who desire such a peep through Mr. Browning's window as this, the shutters are at last by his own courtesy taken down.

Mr. Robert Browning was born at Camberwell, a southern suburb of London, on the 7th of May, 1812. His father, who bore the same name as himself, and who died in 1866 at the age of eighty-four, was in many ways a remarkable man. It is, we must suppose, not merely filial piety that makes his son declare that his father had more true poetic genius than he has. Of course the world at large will answer, " By their fruits shall ye know them," and of palpable fruit in the way of published verse the elder Mr. Browning has nothing to show. But it seems that his force and fluency in the use of the heroic couplet, the only metrical form for which he had much taste, were extraordinary; and his son speaks of his moral vein as that of a Pope born out of due time. For his son's poetic gods he had, of course, no fondness, and, from the very first, the two minds diverged upon every intellectual point, — until the close of the old gentleman's life, when it is pathetic to hear that he learned, as the world was learning, to appreciate the fine flavor of his son's poetry. He was always, however, loving and sympathetic, divining the genuine poetic impulse though blind to the beauty of the forms it took, and in this one case the rare phenomenon seems to have appeared of a boy consciously, and of set purpose, trained to be a poet.

The only other instance that occurs to me is that of Jean Chapelain, who was set apart from birth by his parents "to relight the torch of Malherbe;" the result was not nearly so happy as in the case of Mr. Browning.

The latter, however, can hardly remember a time when his intention was not to be eminent in rhyme, and he began to write at least as early as Cowley. His sister remembers him, as a very little boy, walking round and round the dining-room table, and spanning out the scansion of his verses with his hand on the smooth mahogany. When he was about eight years old, this ambitious young person disdained the narrow field of poetry, and, while retaining that sceptre, debated within himself, as Dryden says Anne Killegrew did, whether he should invade and conquer the province of painting or that of music.

It soon became plain to him, however, that, as he himself put it thirty-five years later,

" I shall never, in the years remaining,
　Paint you pictures, no, nor carve you statues,
　Make you music that should all-express me :
　. . . Verse alone, one life allows me,"

and he began writing with assiduity. It is curious to reflect that all the giants were alive in those days — not even Keats himself laid to sleep under the Roman grasses.

In 1824, the year that Byron died, the boy had collected poems enough to form a volume, and these were taken around to publisher after publisher, but in vain. The first people who saw the nascent genius of this lad of twelve years old were the two Misses Flower, the younger afterward authoress of *Vivia Perpetua*, and too sadly known as Sarah Flower Adams. The elder

Miss Flower thought the poems so remarkable that she copied them and showed them to the distinguished Unitarian, the Rev. William Johnson Fox, then already influential as a radical politician of the finer order. As a matter of course, Mr. Fox was too judicious to recommend the publication of poems so juvenile, but he ventured to prophesy a splendid future for the boy, and he kept the transcripts in his possession. To Mr. Browning's great amusement, after the death of Mr. Fox, in 1864, his daughter, Mrs. Bridell-Fox, returned the MS. to the author, who read in maturity the forgotten verses of his childhood. At the time they were written he was entirely under the influence of Byron, and his verse was so full and melodious that Mr. Fox confessed, long afterward, that he had thought that his snare would be a too gorgeous scale of

language and tenuity of thought, concealed by metrical audacity. But about
a year after this, an event revolution-
ized Robert Browning's whole concep-
tion of poetic art. There came into
his hands a miserable pirated edition of
part of Shelley's works; the window
was dull, but he looked through it into
an enchanted garden. He was impatient to walk there himself, but, in
1825, it was by no means easy to obtain
the books of Shelley. No bookseller
that was applied to knew the name, although Shelley had been dead three
years. At last, inquiry was made of
the editor of the *Literary Gazette*, and
it was replied that the books in question could be obtained of C. & J. Ollier,
of Vere street.

To Vere street, accordingly, Mrs.
Browning proceeded, and brought back
as a present for her son, not only all the

works of Shelley, but three volumes written by a Mr. John Keats, which were recommended to her as being very much in the spirit of Mr. Shelley. A bibliophile of to-day is almost dazed in thinking of the prize which the unconscious lady brought back with her to Camberwell. There was the Pisa *Adonais*, in its purple paper cover; there was *Epipsychidion*, — in short, all the books she bought were still in their first edition, except *The Cenci*, which professed to be in the second. Poets of our own day need not grumble at the indifference of the public, when we see that within human memory two of the greatest writers of modern times, three and four years after their decease, were still utterly unsalable. Well, the dust of the dead Keats and Shelley turned to flower-seed in the brain of the young poet, and very soon wrought a change in the whole of his ambition. First of all, they made him thoroughly dissatisfied with what he had hitherto written, and showed him — always a very salutary lesson for a boy — that the elements of his art were still to be learned. Meanwhile, the business of ordinary education took up the main part of his time ; till 1826, he was at school at Dulwich, then with a tutor at home, and finally, but only for a very short time, at London University.

The elder Mr. Browning had but two children, — the poet, and a daughter who kept house for her brother in his closing years. When the son had arrived at that age at which the bias or opportunity of parents usually dictates a profession to a youth, Mr. Browning asked his son what he intended to be. It was known to the latter that his sister was provided for, and that there would always be

enough to keep him also, and he had
the singular courage to decline to be
rich.   He appealed to his father whether
it would not be better for him to see
life in the best sense, and cultivate the
˙powers of his mind, than to shackle himself in the very outset of his career by
a laborious training, foreign to that
aim.   The wisdom or unwisdom of such
a step is proved by its measure of success.   In the case of Mr. Browning the
determination has never been regretted,
and so great was the confidence of the
father in the genius of the son that the
former at once acquiesced in the pro-
posal.   At this time, young Browning's
brain was full of colossal schemes of
poems.   It is interesting˙and curious to
learn that at a time of life when almost
every poet, whatever his ultimate des-
tination, is trying his power of wing in
song, Mr. Browning, the early Byronic

lilt having been thrown aside, did not attempt any lyrical exercise. He planned a series of monodramatic epics, narratives of the life of typical souls, — a gigantic scheme at which a Victor Hugo or a Lope de Vega would start back aghast.

Several of these great poems were sketched ; only one exists, and that in fragmentary form. At Richmond, whither the family had gone to live, — on the 22d of October, 1832, — Mr. Browning finished a poem which he named, from the object, not the subject, *Pauline.* This piece was read and admired at home, and one day his aunt said to the young man : —

" I hear, Robert, that you have written a poem ; here is the money to print it."

Accordingly, in January, 1833, there went to press, anonymously, a little book of seventy pages, which remained virtually unrecognized until the author, to preserve it from piracy, unwillingly received it among the acknowledged children of his muse, in 1867.

But, although *Pauline* was excluded from recognition by its author for more than thirty years, he has to confess that its production was attended with circumstances of no little importance to him. It was the intention and desire of Mr. Browning that the authorship should remain entirely unknown, but Miss Flower told the secret to Mr. Fox, who reviewed the poem with great warmth and fullness in the *Monthly Repository*. But a more curious incident was that a copy fell into the hands of John Stuart Mill, who was only six years the senior of the poet. It delighted him in the highest degree, and he immediately wrote to the editor of

Tait's Magazine, the only periodical in which he was at that time free to express himself, for leave to review *Pauline* at length. The reply was that nothing would have been more welcome, but that, unfortunately, in the preceding number the poem had been dismissed with one line of contemptuous neglect. Mr. Mill's opportunities extended no further than this one magazine, but at his death there came into Mr. Browning's possession this identical copy, the blank pages of which were crowded with Mill's annotations and remarks. The late John Forster took such an interest in this volume that he borrowed it, — " convey, the wise it call," — and when he died, it passed with his library into the possession of the South Kensington Museum, where the curious relic of the youth of two eminent men has at last found a rest-

ing-place. Nor was this the only instance in which the poem, despite its
anonymity and its rawness, touched a
kindred chord in a man of genius.
There was much in it that was new,
forcible, and fine, — such passages of
description as this of the wood where
Pauline and her lover met: —

" Walled in with a sloped mound of matted shrubs,
Dark, tangled, old and green, still sloping down
To a small pool whose waters lie asleep
Amid the trailing boughs turned water-plants;
And tall trees overarch to keep us in,
Breaking the sunbeams into emerald shafts,
And in the dreamy water one small group
Of two or three strange trees are got together,
Wondering at all around, as strange beasts herd
Together far from their own land : all wildness,
No turf nor moss, for boughs and plants pave all,
And tongues of bank go shelving in the lymph,
Where the pale-throated snake reclines his head,
And old gray stones lie making eddies there,
The wild mice cross them dry-shod : deeper in !
Shut thy soft eyes — now look — still deeper in !
This is the very heart of the woods, all round

Mountain-like heaped above us ; yet even here
One pond of water gleams ; far off the river
Sweeps like a sea, barred out from land ; but one —
One thin clear sheet has overleaped and wound
Into this silent depth, which gained, it lies
Still, as but let by sufferance ; *the trees bend*
O'er it as wild men watch a sleeping girl," —

or such fine bursts of versification as
this about Andromeda : —

" As she awaits the snake on the wet beach,
By the dark rock and the white wave just breaking
At her feet ; quite naked and alone ; a thing
You doubt not, fear not for, secure that God
Will come in thunder from the stars to save her."

Such beauties as these were not likely
to escape the notice of curious lovers
of poetry. Many years after, when Mr.
Browning was living in Florence, he
received a letter from a young painter
whose name was quite unknown to him,
asking him whether he were the author
of a poem called *Pauline*, which was
somewhat in his manner, and which the

writer had so greatly admired that he had transcribed the whole of it in the British Museum reading-room. The letter was signed D. G. Rossetti, and thus began Mr. Browning's acquaintance with this eminent man. But to the world at large *Pauline* was a sealed book, by nobody, and the reviewers simply ignored it.

One very creditable exception was the *Athenæum*, then in its infancy, which dedicated several columns to a kindly, if not very profound, analysis, and to copious quotations. Mr. Browning discovered long afterward that this notice was written by Allan Cunningham.

After the publication of *Pauline* there came a period of respite, in which the poetical ferment of the young writer's mind was settling down, and his genius was preparing to take its proper

form. The scheme of illustrating, in a
series of vast biographies in blank verse,
whatever was unusual or tragical in the
history of a soul, was gradually aban-
doned, and the excitement of travel took
the place of the excitement of composition. Mr. Browning set out upon his
Wanderjahr, 1834, and made a long
stay at St. Petersburg. Of all that
was thought and planned in these two
years preceding the rapid authorship of
Paracelsus, the only specimen remaining is to be found in four interesting
lyrics, included in the *Dramatic Lyrics*
of 1842, and now finally relegated to
Men and Women. Two of these were
printed first in Fox's *Monthly Repository*, under the single title of "Mad-
house Cells," although they are now
known to every reader of Mr. Browning
as "Joannes Agricola in Meditation"
and "Porphyria's Lover." It is a curi-

ous matter for reflection that two poems
so unique in their construction and con-
ception, so modern, so interesting, so
new, could be printed without attract-
ing attention, so far as it would appear,
from any living creature.   Mr. Browning's other contributions to the *Monthly
Repository* were the song, now inserted
in *Pippa Passes*, beginning : —

> " A King lived long ago,
>   In the morning of the world,
>   When earth was nigher heaven than now,"

and the following sonnet,[1] which has
not been reprinted in any edition of the
poet's works : —

> "Eyes, calm beside thee (Lady couldst thou know!),
>   May turn away thick with fastgathering tears :
> I glance not where all gaze : thrilling and low
>   Their passionate praises reach thee — my cheek
>   wears

[1] I owe the identification of this sonnet, which
Mr. Browning had forgotten, to Mrs. Bridell-Fox.

Alone no wonder when thou passest by ;
Thy tremulous lids, bent and suffused, reply
To the irrepressible homage which doth glow
  On every lip but mine : if in thine ears
Their accents linger — and thou dost recall
  Me as I stood, still, guarded, very pale,
  Beside each votarist whose lighted brow
Wore worship like an aureole, ' O'er them all
  My beauty,' thou wilt murmur, ' did prevail
  Save that one only ' : — Lady, couldst thou
    know ! ' ''

August 17, 1834.

Here was a poet with a fresh voice, appealing to the intellectual youth of Europe in a direct way, such as only one other man had dreamed of, and that was Heine.

Then came *Paracelsus*, written in London through the winter of 1834, finished in March, 1835, and published before the summer. This work has had so many admirers that it needs, perhaps, a little courage to say that it was surely not so important as a sign of its author's genius as the little pieces just mentioned. It is a drama of a shapeless kind, parent in this sort of a monstrous family of *Festuses*, and *Balders*, and *Life Dramas*, only quite lately extirpated, and never any more, it is hoped, to flourish above ground. There are four persons in the drama: Paracelsus, the male and female genii of his career; Festus and Michal, friend and lover; and finally Aprile, the foil and counterpoise to his ambitious gravity. Every one knows how the poem is conducted; how full it is of subtlety, of melody, of eloquent and casuistical intelligence. But we cannot forget that it is a drama in which one of the characters, more than once, expresses himself in upward of three hundred lines of unbroken soliloquy. The precedent was bad, as all disregard of the canons of artistic form is apt to be; and in the hands of his imitators Mr. Browning must often have shuddered at his own contorted reflection. The public refused to have anything to say to so strange a poem; very few copies were sold, and the reviews were contemptuously adverse. The *Athenæum*, even, which had received *Pauline* so warmly, dismissed *Paracelsus* with a warning to the author that it was useless to reproduce the obscurity of Shelley minus his poetic beauty.

But certain finer minds here and there recognized the treasury of power and genius concealed in this crabbed shape. The *Examiner*, in particular, contained a review of the poem at great length, in which full justice was done to Mr. Browning's genius. This, again, was the commencement of a memorable intimacy. But in the meantime the young poet formed the acquaintance of one of the most striking personages of that generation — Macready, the tragedian. This happened at a dinner at the house of W. J. Fox, on the 27th of November, 1835. The actor was exceedingly charmed with the young and ardent writer, who, he said, looked more like a poet than any man he had ever met. He read *Paracelsus* with a sort of ecstasy, and cultivated Mr. Browning's acquaintance on every occasion. He asked him to spend New Year's Day with him at his country-house at Elstree, and on the last day of 1835, Mr. Browning found himself at "The Blue Posts" waiting for the coach, in company with two or three other persons, who looked at him with curiosity. One of these, a tall, ardent, noticeable young fellow, constantly caught his eye, but as the strangers knew one another, and as Mr. Browning knew none of them, no conversation passed as they drove northward. It turned out that they were all Macready's guests, one of the elder men being George Cattermole, while the noticeable youth was no other than John Forster. He, on being introduced to Mr. Browning, said: "Did you see a little notice of you I wrote in the *Examiner?* The friendship so begun lasted, with a certain interval, until the end of Forster's life.

The acquaintance with Macready deepened rapidly on both sides. The actor had scarcely finished reading *Paracelsus* before he began to think that here was a tragic poet to his mind. He suggested that Mr. Browning should write him an acting play, and the subject of Narses, the eunuch who conquered Italy for Justinian, was discussed between them. At first the actor seemed more eager in the matter than the poet.

Early in 1836, Macready made this striking entry in his journal: —

"Browning said that I had *bit* him by my performance of *Othello*, and I told him I hoped I should make the blood come. It would, indeed, be some recompense for the miseries, the humiliations, the heart-sickening disgusts which I have endured in my profession, if, by its exercise, I had awakened a spirit of poetry whose influence would elevate, ennoble, and adorn our degraded drama. May it be!"

In April, 1836, the miseries to which Macready referred, and which were caused by the meanness of his manager and the bad state of the law of contract, were suddenly brought to a culmination. One evening, after playing part of *Richard II.*, and being forbidden to conclude the tragedy, Macready's patience suddenly failed him, and he inflicted upon the notorious and ridiculous Mr.

Alfred Bunn a sound thrashing. Not-
withstanding this unfortunate *contre-
temps*, to which Mr. Macready's chival-
rous ideal gave more importance in his
own eyes than was felt by an indulgent
and scandal-loving public, it was possible, as early as May 26th, 1836, to
bring out at Covent Garden Theatre,
under the management of Mr. Osbaldiston, Talfourd's new tragedy of *Ion*.
The supper which succeeded the first
performance of this extremely successful
play was a momentous occasion to Mr.
Browning. He found himself seated
opposite to Macready, who was sup-
ported on his right hand and his left
by two elderly gentlemen, in whom
the young poet recognized for the first
time William Wordsworth and Walter
Savage Landor. In the course of the
evening Talfourd, with marked kind-
ness, proposed the name of the youngest

English poet, and Wordsworth, lean-
ing across the table, said, with august
affability, "I am proud to drink your
health, Mr. Browning!" The latter
saw much of Wordsworth during the
next few years, for Talfourd invited
him to his house whenever Wordsworth
came up to town. He listened to his
slow talk with reverence and interest,
but never got over the somewhat chill-
ing and awful personal bearing of the
old man. With Landor, on the con-
trary, Mr. Browning afterward became,
as readers of Forster's life must be
aware, extremely intimate, and helped,
indeed, to add sunshine to the last dark
days of that leonine exile. To return,
however, to the "Ion" supper: the
success of that tragedy had whetted the
appetite of all the luckless playwrights
of the day, and one of them, Miss Mit-
ford, with pert audacity, ventured to

propose a poetic play to the tragedian
while he was at table. But she utterly
failed in her ruse, and Mr. Browning
was, therefore, doubly surprised when,
as the guests were leaving, Macready
came behind him on the stairs, and, lay-
ing his hand on his arm, said, " Write
a play, Browning, and keep me from
going to America ! " It was said so
earnestly that there could be no doubt
that it was meant, and Mr. Browning
simply replied, " Shall it be historical
and English ? What do you say to a
drama on Strafford ? " In this rapid
interchange of sympathies Mr. Browning's next work was conceived, but it
was several months before he satisfied
himself that he was sufficiently read in
the historical part of the subject to fill
up the plot. On the 19th of November, 1836, the tragedy of *Strafford* was
brought, almost finished, to Macready ;

in March of the next year it was com-
pleted and put in rehearsal, and, on the
first of May, it was brought out on the
boards of Covent Garden Theatre.

It is time now to deny a statement
that has been repeated *ad nauseam* in
every notice that professes to give an account of Mr. Browning's career. Whatever is said or not said, it is always remarked that his plays have "failed" on
the stage. In point of fact, the three
plays which he has brought out have all
succeeded, and have owed it to fortui-
tous circumstances that their tenure
on the boards has been comparatively
short. *Strafford* was produced when
the finances of Covent Garden Theatre
were at their lowest ebb, and nothing
was done to give dignity or splendor to
the performance. "Not a rag for the
new tragedy," said Mr. Osbaldiston.
The king was taken by Mr. Dale, who

was stone-deaf, and who acted so badly that, as one of the critics said, it was a pity that the pit did not rise as one man and push him off the stage. All sorts of alterations were made in the text; where the poet spoke of "grave gray eyes," the manager corrected it in rehearsal to "black eyes." But at last Macready appeared, in the second scene of the second act, in more than his wonted majesty, crossing and recrossing the stage like one of Vandyke's courtly personages come to life again, and Miss Helen Faucit threw such tenderness and passion into the part of Lady Carlisle as surpassed all that she had previously displayed of histrionic power. Under these circumstances, and in spite of the dull acting of Vandenhoff, who played Pym without any care or interest, the play was well received on the first night, and on the second night was applauded with enthusiasm by a crowded house. There was every expectation that the tragedy would have no less favorable a " run " than *Ion* had enjoyed, but after five nights, Vandenhoff suddenly withdrew, and though Elton volunteered to take his place, the financial condition of the theatre, in spite of the undiminished popularity of the piece, put an end to its representation.

Mr. Browning, the elder, had paid for the cost of *Paracelsus ; Strafford* was taken by Longmans, and brought out, at their expense, as a little volume, — not, like most of the tragedies of the day, in dark-gray paper covers, with a white label. However, at that time the public absolutely declined to buy Mr. Browning's books, and *Strafford*, although more respectfully received by the press, was as great a financial failure as *Paracelsus*. It was part of Mr.

Browning's essentially masculine order
of mind to be in no wise disheartened
or detached from his purpose by this
indifference of the public.   He was
silent for three years, but all the time
busy with copious production.   The success of *Strafford* on the stage led Mr.
Browning's thoughts very naturally to
the drama, and besides the purely lyrical
masque or "proverb" of *Pippa Passes*,
he concluded, before 1840, two tragedies
with the intention of seeing them acted.
These were *King Victor and King
Charles*, and *Mansoor the Hierophant*,
rebaptized on publication by the name
of *The Return of the Druses*.   These
plays, however, found no manager or
publisher willing to accept them, and
the author fell back on the dream that
he had commenced his career with,
namely, that of chronicling in poetry
the whole life of a single soul.   He set

to work, and produced one of the most considerable, certainly one of the most characteristic, of his works, in the epic of *Sordello*, begun in 1838, finished and printed in 1840. It is scarcely necessary to remark that for forty years this book has been an eminent stumbling-block, not merely in the path of fools, but in that of very sensible and cultivated people. "The entirely unintelligible *Sordello*" has enjoyed at least its due share of obloquy and neglect. There are not a few of Mr. Browning's readers who would miss it from the collection of his books more than any other of his longer poems. It possesses passages of melody and insight, fresh enough, surprising enough to form the whole stock-in-trade of a respectable poet; it needs reading three times, but on the third even a school-boy of tolerable intelligence will find it luminous, if not entirely lucid, and half the charge of obscurity is really a confession of indolence and inattention.

"Who wills may hear 'Sordello's' story told,"

and if our space to-day would give us leave to roam through its fragrant pages, we might find a thousand reasons why *Sordello* ought to be one of the most readable of books.

And yet the Naddos of contemporary criticism were not wholly wrong. The book is difficult, and Mr. Browning in the philosophic afternoon of life frankly confesses as much. It is hard reading, over-condensed, over-rapid, like much of Milton in its too arrogant contempt for the commonplace habits of the intelligence. This is the author's explanation of his error, for that it was an error he is perhaps more ready than some of his admirers to admit. In 1838, the condition of English poetry was singularly tame and namby-pamby.   Tennyson's voice was only heard by a few.   The many delighted in poor " L. E. L.," whose sentimental " golden violets " and gushing *improvvisatores* had found a tragic close at Cape Coast Castle. Among living poets, the most popular were good old James Montgomery, droning on at his hopeless insipidities and graceful " goodnesses," the Hon. Mrs. Norton, a sort of soda-water Byron, and poor, rambling T. K. Hervey.   The plague of annuals and books of beauty was on the land, with its accompanying flood of verses by Alaric A. Watts and " Delta " Moir.   These virtuous and now almost forgotten poetasters, had brought the art of poetry into such disesteem, with their puerilities and their thin, diluted sentiment, that verse was beginning to be considered unworthy of exercise by a serious or original thinker. Into this ocean of thin soup Mr. Browning threw his small square of solid pemmican, — a little mass which could have supplied ideas and images to a dozen "L. E. L.'s" without losing much of its consistence. Of course, to a generation long fed on such thin diet, the new contribution seemed much more like a stone than like anything edible, and even to this day there are lovers of poetry who can get as little out of it as Alton Locke could. About 1863, Mr. Browning, becoming a little impatient of the long-repeated denigration of his favorite offspring, set about rewriting *Sordello* on a simpler principle; needless to say that was a failure, and there are few who will regret that for once, at least, so profound a student of the human heart wrote rather as he himself felt than as his readers, even the most

sympathetic of them, might have wished.
The book has become a classic, and to
each coming generation will in all prob-
ability present less difficulty than to the
preceding one.

But from the popular point of view
Sordello was a failure, and in the face
of so much poetry still unprinted, Mr.
Browning could not but ruefully remember how expensive his books had been
to his sympathetic and uncomplaining
father. To go on indefinitely in this
way was scarcely to be thought of, and
yet poetry kept in a desk, on the Hora-
tian principle, is a property that wears
out the soul with hope deferred. One
day, as the poet was discussing the matter with Mr. Edward Moxon, the publisher, the latter remarked that at that
time he was bringing out some editions
of the old Elizabethan dramatists in a
comparatively cheap form, and that if

Mr. Browning would consent to print his poems as pamphlets, using this cheap ,type, the expense would be very inconsiderable. The poet jumped at the idea, and it was agreed that each poem should form a separate brochure of just one sheet, — sixteen pages, in double columns, — the entire cost of which should not exceed twelve or fifteen pounds. In this fashion began the celebrated series of *Bells and Pomegranates*, eight numbers of which, a perfect treasury of fine poetry, came out successively between 1841 and 1846. *Pippa Passes* led the way, and was priced first at sixpence ; then, the sale being inconsiderable, at a shilling, which greatly encouraged the sale ; and so, slowly, up to half a crown, at which the price of each number finally rested. As the advertisement of *Bells and Pomegranates* has never been reprinted, and as that volume is not very common, I make no apology for reproducing that characteristic little document : —

" Two or three years ago I wrote a play, about which the chief matter I much care to recollect at present is, that a pitfull of good-natured people applauded it. Ever since, I have been desirous of doing something in the same way that should better reward their attention. What follows I mean for the first of a series of dramatical pieces, to come out at intervals, and I amuse myself by fancying that the cheap mode in which they appear will for once help me to a sort of pit-audience again. Of course, such a work must go on no longer than it is liked ; and to provide against a certain and but too possible contingency, let me hasten to say now what, if I were sure of success, I would try to say circumstantially enough at the close, that I dedicate my best intentions most admiringly to the author of *Ion*, — most affectionately to Serjeant Talfourd."

There had been nothing in the pastoral kind written so delightfully as *Pippa Passes* since the days of the Jacobean dramatists. It was inspired by the same feeling as gave charm and freshness to the masques of Day and Nabbes, but it was carried out with a mastery of execution and fullness of knowledge such as those unequal writers could not dream of exercising. The figure of Pippa herself, the unconscious messenger of good spiritual tidings to so many souls in dark places, is one of the most beautiful that Mr. Browning has produced, and in at least one of the more serious scenes, — that between Sebald and Ottima, — he reaches a tragic height that places him on a level with the greatest modern dramatists. Of the lyrical interludes and seed-pearls of song scattered through the scenes, it is a commonplace to say that nothing more exquisite or natural was ever written, or rather warbled. The public was first won to Mr. Browning by *Pippa Passes*. Next year, 1842, he printed the old tragedy of *King Victor and King Charles*, which he had had by him for some years. If *Pippa Passes* was, as Miss Barrett said, a pomegranate that showed

"A heart within blood-tinctured, of a veined humanity,"

this latter drama was a bell, clear-toned and clangorous, fitly rung before the curtain should rise upon a stately theatrical spectacle. The poetry here, as in *Strafford*, which it resembles, is carefully subordinated to stage effect and movement, and it is unfortunate that Mr. Browning was not successful in getting it accepted by any manager, for it would be a popular piece on the stage. Not a lyrical passage, scarcely a lyrical touch, checks the business and bustle of the scenes till Victor dies so majestically, with his son's crown on his head, defying d'Ormea. The same year followed the brief pamphlet or booklet called *Dramatic Lyrics*. Short as this book is, only sixteen pages, it was shorter still when the printer's devil came from Mr. Moxon's shop to ask for more copy to fill up the sheet. Mr. Browning gave him a *jeu d'esprit* which he had written to amuse little Willie Macready, and which he had had no idea of publishing. This was *The Pied Piper of Hamelin*, which has probably introduced its author's name into hundreds of thousands of homes where otherwise it never would have penetrated. In other respects the collection was sparse, but remarkable enough. First came the three " Cavalier Tunes," as at present; then, under

the titles of " Italy " and " France,"
what we now find among the *Dramatic
Romances* as " My Last Duchess " and
" Count Gismond." Then the " Incident of the French Camp " and " The
Soliloquy of the Spanish Cloister " ;
then " In a Gondola," perhaps the most
delicate in harmonic effect of all Mr.
Browning's lyrics ; then " Artemis Pro-
logizes " ; then " Waring," in which
was sung the disappearance of Mr. Alfred Dommett, who, after a long exile,
returned from Vishnuland, or New Zea-
land, a few years ago ; then " Rudel
and the Lady of Tripoli," " Cristina,"
" Mad-house Cells," — which we have
already discussed, — " Through the Me-
tidja," and finally " The Pied Piper."
Early in 1843 there followed the glow-
ing and passionate tragedy *The Return
of the Druses*, a play which would be
sure to rivet attention on the stage, but

which no manager hitherto has had the courage to produce.

But, in the meantime, the hopes that had sprung eternal in the breasts of all dramatic poets began to cluster once more around the person of Mr. Macready. That illustrious actor, by that time recognized as by far the most able and eminent tragedian in the English-speaking world, after performing for a season at the Haymarket, took Drury Lane Theatre under his own management, and held out flattering promises to the poets. This season opened on the 10th of December, 1842, with *The Patrician's Daughter* of Mr. Westland Marston. This was the first work of a young man of great promise, of whom much had been talked in literary and theatrical circles. Mr. Macready took the part of Mordaunt, Miss Helen Faucit that of Lady Mabel Lynterne, and great pains were taken to secure a thoroughly satisfactory cast. It was distinctly understood that if *The Patrician's Daughter* was a great success, the public was to be rewarded by a series of original tragedies by poets of repute. Everything seemed as glittering and auspicious as possible, and nobody knew what a dangerous game Macready was playing. He was, as a matter of fact, on the verge of bankruptcy, and driven almost to distraction by a variety of vexations. Unfortunately, Marston's play, from which so much was expected, enjoyed only a success of esteem. It was removed, to be succeeded on the boards by a play called *Plighted Troth*, by a brother of George Darley, and a man of the same peevish, hopeless temperament as his more distinguished relative. This tragedy proved to be miserable trash, and was scarcely endured

a single night. But, in the meantime,
Mr. Browning, who had been asked by
Macready to write a play for him, had
devised and composed, in the space of
five days, one of the most remarkable
of his works, *A Blot in the 'Scutcheon*. This had been received, and
delight had been expressed by Macready on reading it. The author was,
therefore, surprised that, on the with-
drawal of *Plighted Troth*, he received
no invitation, in accordance with eti-
quette, to read it aloud to the actors
previous to rehearsal. He had no ink-
ling whatever of Macready's embarrass-
ments, and not the slightest notion that
it was hoped that he would withdraw
the piece. At last, on Saturday, the
4th of February, 1843, Macready called
Mr. Browning into his private room,
and said to him : —

"Your play was read to the actors

yesterday, and they received it with shouts of laughter."

" Who read it ? "

" Oh, Mr. Wilmot."

Now, Wilmot was the prompter, a broadly comic personage with a wooden leg and a very red face, whose vulgar sallies were the delight of all the idle jesters that hung about the theatre. That such a drama as *A Blot in the 'Scutcheon* should be given to Wilmot to read was simply an insult, and one of which Mr. Browning did not conceal his perception. Macready saw his mistake, and said : " Wilmot is a ridiculous being, of course. On Monday I myself will read it to the actors." On Monday, accordingly, he read it, but he announced to Mr. Browning that he should not act in it himself, but that Phelps, then quite a new man, would take the principal part. This was an

unheard-of thing in those days, when it
was supposed that Macready was absolutely essential to a new tragedy. Of
course his hope was that Mr. Browning would say: " You not play in it?
Then, of course, I withdraw it." But
the actor's manner was so far from sug-
gesting that truth that the poet never
suspected the real state of the case.
He accepted Phelps, but, when the rehearsal began on Tuesday, Phelps was
very ill with English cholera, and could
not be present, so Macready read his
part for him. On Wednesday Mr.
Browning noticed that Macready was
not merely reading : he was rehearsing
the part, moving across the stage, and
counting his steps. When Mr. Browning arrived on Thursday, there was
poor Phelps sitting close to the door, as
white as a sheet, evidently very poorly.
Macready began : " As Mr. Phelps is

so ill — you are very ill, are you not,
Mr. Phelps? — it will be impossible for
him to master his part by Saturday, and
I shall therefore take it myself." Mr.
Browning was not at all pleased with
this shuffling, for which he could divine
no cause, and he was still more annoyed
at the changes which were being made
in the poem. The title was to be
changed to " The Sisters," the first act
was to be cut out, and it was to end
without any tragic *finale*, but with these
sublime lines, due to the unaided genius
of Macready himself :

" Within a monastery's solitude,
Penance and prayer shall wear **my life away.**"

Mr. Browning was determined, if possible, to check this wanton sacrifice of
the poem, and so he took the MS. to
his publisher Moxon, who also had a
quarrel with Macready, and who was
therefore only too pleased to coöper-

ate in his confusion. *A Blot in the 'Scutcheon* was printed in a few hours, in a single sheet, as part five of *Bells and Pomegranates*, and was in the hands of each of the actors before Mr. Browning reached the theatre on Friday morning. As he entered, he met Phelps, who was waiting for him at the door, and who said:

"It is true, sir, that I have been ill, but I am better now, and if you chose to give the part to me, which I can hardly expect you to do, I should be able to act it to-morrow night."

"But is it possible," said Mr. Browning, "that you could learn it so soon?"

"Yes," answered Phelps, "I should sit up all night and know it perfectly."

Mr. Browning's determination was soon taken; he took Phelps with him into the green-room, where Macready was already studying the play in its printed form, with the actors around him. Mr. Browning stopped him, and said :

" I find that Mr. Phelps, although he has been ill, feels himself quite able to take the part, and I shall be very glad to leave it in his hands." Macready rose and said :

" But do you understand that I, *I*, am going to act the part? "

" I shall be very glad to intrust it to Mr. Phelps," said Mr. Browning, upon which Macready crumpled up the play he was holding in his hand, and threw it to the other end of the room.

After such an event, it was with no very hopeful feelings that Mr. Browning awaited the first performance on the next night, February 11th. He would not allow his parents or his sister to go to the theatre ; no tickets were sent to him, but finding that the stage-box was

his, not by favor, but by right, he went
with no other companion than Mr. Edward Moxon. But his expectations of
failure were not realized. Phelps acted
magnificently, carrying out the remark
of Macready, that the difference between himself and the other actors was
that they could do magnificent things
now and then, on a spurt, but that he
could always command his effects. Anderson, a *jeune premier* of promise,
acted the young lover with considerable
spirit, although the audience was not
quite sure whether to laugh or no when
he sang his song, " There 's a Woman
like a Dewdrop," in the act of climbing
in at the window. Finally, Miss Helen
Faucit almost surpassed herself in Mil-
dred Tresham. The piece was entirely
successful, though Mr. R. H. Horne,
who was in the front of the pit, tells me
that Anderson was for some time only

half-serious, and quite ready to have
turned traitor if the public had encouraged him. When the curtain went
down, the applause was vociferous.
Phelps was called and recalled, and
then there rose the cry of " Author ! "
To this Mr. Browning remained silent
and out of sight, and the audience con-
tinued to shout until Anderson came
forward, and keeping his eye on Mr.
Browning, said, " I believe that the author is not present, but if he is I entreat
him to come forward ! " The poet,
however, turned a deaf ear to this ap-
peal, and went home very sore with
Macready, and what he considered his
purposeless and vexatious schemings.
A Blot in the 'Scutcheon was announced to be played " three times a
week until further notice " ; was per-
formed with entire success to crowded
houses, until the final collapse of Ma-

cready's schemes brought it abruptly to a close.

Such is the true story of an event on which Macready, in his journals, has kept an obstinate silence, and which one erring critic after another has chronicled as the failure, " as a matter of course," of Mr. Browning's " improbable " play. Neither on its first appearance, nor when Phelps revived it at Sadler's Wells, was *A Blot in the 'Scutcheon* received by the public otherwise than with warm applause. As in the case of *Strafford*, a purely accidental circumstance, unconnected with Mr. Browning, cut it short in the midst of a successful run.

Fired with the memory of so many plaudits, Mr. Browning set himself to the composition of another actable play, and this also had its little hour of success, though not until many years afterward. *Colombe's Birthday*, which formed number six of *Bells and Pomegranates*, appeared in 1843. I have before me at the present moment a copy of the first edition, marked for acting by the author, who has written: " I made the alterations in this copy to suit some — I forget what — projected stage representation : not that of Miss Faucit, which was carried into effect long afterward." The stage directions are numerous and minute, showing the science which the dramatist had gained since he first essayed to put his creations on the boards. Some of the suggestions are characteristic enough. For instance, " unless a very good Valence " is found, this extremely fine speech, perhaps the jewel of the play, is to be left out. In the present editions the verses run otherwise. Valence speaks :

" He stands, a man, now; stately, strong and
    wise —
One great aim, like a guiding-star, before —
Which tasks strength, wisdom, stateliness to fol-
    low,
As, not its substance, but its shine, he tracks,
Nor dreams of more than, just evolving these
To fullness, will suffice him to life's end.
After this star, out of a night he springs,
A beggar's cradle for the throne of thrones
He quits; so mounting, feels each step he mounts,
Nor as from each to each exultingly
He passes, overleaps one grain of joy.
This for his own good : — with the world each gift
Of God and man — Reality, Tradition,
Fancy, and Fact — so well environ him,
That as a mystic panoply they serve —
Of force untenanted to awe mankind,
And work his purpose out with half the world,
While he, their master, dexterously slipt
From such encumbrance, is meantime employed
In his own prowess with the other half.
So shall he go on, every day's success
Adding, to what is He, a solid strength, —
An airy might to what encircles him,
Till at the last, so life's routine shall grow,
That as the Emperor only breathes and moves,

His shadow shall be watched, his step or stalk
Become a comfort or a portent ; how
He trails his ermine take significance, —
Till even his power shall cease his power to be,
And most his weakness men shall fear, nor van-
        quish
Their typified invincibility.
So shall he go on greatening, till **he ends** —
The man of men, the spirit of all flesh,
The fiery centre of an earthy world ! "

Mr. Browning says that very little has hitherto been printed about his life, and that little " mostly false." A curious instance of this last clause is the statement that has been authoritatively made, in a quarter from which we do not expect error, to the effect that *Colombe's Birthday* was brought out by Miss Cushman, at the Haymarket, in 1844, as *The Duchess of Cleves*. The editor of Mr. Browning's letters to Mr. R. H. Horne was probably thinking about a play, with a " Duchess " in

the title, written by Henry Chorley
for Miss Cushman, which she brought
out while Mr. Browning was in Italy.
It seems to have been some projected
performance of *Colombe's Birthday* in
1846, by Helen Faucit, to whom the
poet had read his play, that caused the
latter to make the stage directions to
which I have just referred. In point
of fact, it was not till 1852 that Miss
Faucit produced, and with marked success, the play in question.

The last number of *Bells and Pomegranates*, which appeared in double size,
contained a quaint rabbinical apology
for the general title, and consisted of
two plays, *Luria*, dedicated to Walter
Savage Landor, and *A Soul's Tragedy*.
These bore the date 1846, and with
these the first act of Mr. Browning's
public as well as private life would
seem to have closed, for on the 12th of

September, 1846, he was married, at St. Marylebone, to Miss Elizabeth Barrett Barrett, the illustrious poet, and directly afterward proceeded with her to find a new home in Italy.

April, 1881.

PERSONAL IMPRESSIONS

PERSONAL IMPRESSIONS

THOSE who have frequently seen our revered and beloved friend during the past year will hardly join in the general chorus of surprise which has greeted the death of one so strong in appearance and so hale and green. Rather with these there will be a faint sort of congratulation that such a life, so manifestly waning in essential vigor, should have been spared the indignities of decline, the "cold gradations of decay." For a year past no close observer could have doubted that the robustness which seemed still invincible in the summer of 1888 was rudely shaken. Cold upon cold left the poet weaker; the recuperative power was rapidly and continuously on the decrease. But a little while ago, and to think of Mr. Browning and of illness together seemed impossible. It is a singular fact that he who felt so keenly for human suffering had scarcely known, by experience, what physical pain was. The vigor, the exemption from feebleness, which marks his literary genius, accompanied the man as well. I recollect his giving a picturesque account of a headache he suffered from, once, in St. Petersburg, about the year 1834! Who amongst us is fortunate enough to remember his individual headaches? I seem to see him now, about six years ago, standing in the east wind on the doorstep of his house in Warwick Crescent, declaring with emphasis that he felt ill, really ill, more ill than he had felt for half a century, and looking all the while, in spite of that indisposition, a monument of sturdy health. Even his decline has been the reluctant fall of a wholesome and well-balanced being. Painlessly, without intellectual obscuration, demanding none of that pity that he deprecated, he falls asleep in Italy, faint indeed, yet, to the very last, pursuing. Since those we love must pass away; since the light must sooner or later sink in the lantern, there is, perhaps, no better way than this. We may repeat of him what Sir Thomas Browne said of his friend, " We have missed not our desires in his soft departure, which was scarce an expiration."

It is natural in these first moments to think more of the man than of his works. The latter remain with us, and coming generations will comprehend them better than we do. But our memories of the former, though far less salient, have this importance — that they will pass away with us. Every hour henceforward makes the man more shadowy. We must condense our recollections, if they are not to prove wholly volatile and fugitive. In these few pages, then, I shall mainly strive to contribute my pencil-sketch to the gallery of portraits which will be preserved. He was so many-sided that there may be room for any picture of him that is quite sincere and personal, however slight it may prove; and in the case of Mr. Browning, far more than of most men of genius, the portrait may be truly and boldly drawn without offense. There is no prominent feature of character which has to be slurred over, no trick or foible to be concealed. No man ever showed a more handsome face to private friendship, no one disappointed or repelled less, no one, upon intimate acquaintance, required less to be apologized for or explained away.

There have been many attempts to describe Mr. Browning as a talker in society. One of the best, from the pen of an accomplished observer, appeared last autumn in the *New Review*. But his private conversation was a very different thing from his talk over the dinner-table or in a picture-gallery. It was a very much finer phenomenon, and one which tallied far better with the noble breadth of his genius. To a single listener, with whom he was on familiar terms, the Browning of his own study was to the Browning of a dinner party as a tiger is to a domestic cat. In such conversation his natural strength came out. His talk assumed the volume and the tumult of a cascade. His voice rose to a shout, sank to a whisper, ran up and down the gamut of conversational melody. Those whom he was expecting will never forget his welcome, the loud trumpet-note from

the other end of the passage, the talk
already in full flood at a distance of
twenty feet.   Then, in his own study or
drawing-room, what he loved was to
capture the visitor in a low armchair's
" sofa-lap of leather," and from a most
unfair vantage of height to tyrannize,
to walk around the victim, in front, behind, on this side, on that, weaving
magic circles, now with gesticulating
arms thrown high, now grovelling on
the floor to find some reference in a
folio, talking all the while, a redundant
turmoil of thoughts, fancies, and reminiscences flowing from those generous
lips.   To think of it is to conjure up an
image of intellectual vigor, armed at
every point, but overflowing, none the
less, with the geniality of strength.

The last time that the present writer
enjoyed one of these never-to-be-for-
gotten talks was on the earliest Sunday

in June last summer. For the first
time since many years Mr. Browning
was in Cambridge, and he was much
fêted. He proposed a temporary re-
treat from too full society, and we
retired alone to the most central and
sequestered part of the beautiful Fel-
lows' Garden of Trinity. A little tired
and silent at first, he was no sooner
well ensconced under the shadow of
a tree, in a garden-chair, than his
tongue became unloosed. The blue sky
was cloudless above, summer foliage
hemmed us round in a green mist, a pink
mountain of a double-may in blossom
rose in front. We were close to a hot
shrub of sweetbriar that exhaled its
balm in the sunshine. Commonly given
to much gesticulation, the poet sat quite
still on this occasion ; and, the perfect
quiet being only broken by his voice,
the birds lost fear and came closer and

closer, curiously peeping. So we sat
for more than two hours, and I could
but note what I had had opportunity to
note before, that although, on occasion,
he could be so accurate an observer of
nature, it was not instinctive with him
to observe. In the blaze of summer,
with all the life of birds and insects
moving around us, he did not borrow
an image from or direct an allusion to
any natural fact about us.

He sat and talked of his own early
life and aspirations ; how he marvelled,
as he looked back, at the audacious ob-
stinacy which had made him, when a
youth, determine to be a poet and nothing but a poet. He remarked that all
his life long he had never known what
it was to have to do a certain thing
to-day and not to-morrow ; he thought
this had led to superabundance of production, since, on looking back, he could

see that he had often, in his unfettered
leisure, been afraid to do nothing.
Then, with complete frankness, he de-
scribed the long-drawn desolateness of
his early and middle life as a literary
man ; how, after certain spirits had
seemed to rejoice in his first sprightly
runnings, and especially in *Paracelsus*,
a blight had fallen upon his very admirers. He touched, with a slight irony,
on "the entirely unintelligible *Sordello*," and the forlorn hope of *Bells
and Pomegranates*. Then he fell,
more in the habitual manner of old
men, to stories of early loves and
hatreds, Italian memories of the forties,
stories with names in them that meant
nothing to his ignorant listener. And,
in the midst of these reminiscences, a
chord of extreme interest to the critic
was touched. For in recounting a story
of some Tuscan nobleman who had

shown him two exquisite miniature-paintings, the work of a young artist who should have received for them the prize in some local contest, and who, being unjustly defrauded, broke his ivories, burned his brushes, and indignantly forswore the thankless art for ever, Mr. Browning suddenly reflected that there was, as he said, " stuff for a poem " in that story, and immediately with extreme vivacity began to sketch the form it should take, the suppression of what features and the substitution of what others were needful ; and finally suggested the non-obvious or inverted moral of the whole, in which the act of spirited defiance was shown to be, really, an act of tame renunciation, the poverty of the artist's spirit being proved in his eagerness to snatch, even though it was by honest merit, a benefit simply material.   The poet said, distinctly, that

he had never before reflected on this incident as one proper to be versified ; the
speed, therefore, with which the creative
architect laid the foundations, built the
main fabric, and even put on the domes
and pinnacles of his poem was, no doubt,
of uncommon interest. He left it, in
five minutes, needing nothing but the
mere outward crust of the versification.
It will be a matter of some curiosity to
see whether the poem so started and
sketched was actually brought to com-
pletion.

It cannot have escaped the notice of
any one who knew Robert Browning
well, and who compares him in thought
with other men of genius whom he may
have known, that it was not his strength
only, his vehement and ever-eruptive
force, that distinguished him, but to an
almost equal extent his humanity. Of
all great poets, except (one fancies)

Chaucer, he must have been the most accessible. It is almost a necessity with imaginative genius of a very high order to require support from without : sympathy, admiration, amusement, must be constantly poured in to balance the creative evaporation. But Mr. Browning demanded no such tribute. He rather hastened forward with both hands full of entertainment for the new-comer, anxious to please rather than hoping to be pleased. The most part of men of genius look upon an unknown comer as certainly a bore and probably an enemy, but to Robert Browning the whole world was full of vague possibilities of friendship. No one resented more keenly an unpleasant specimen of humanity, no one could snub more royally at need, no one was — certain premises being established — more ruthless in administering the *coup de grâce;* but then his surprise gave weight to his indignation. He had assumed a new acquaintance to be a good fellow, and behold! against all ordinary experience, he had turned out to be a bore or a sneak. Sudden, irreparable chastisement must fall on one who had proved the poet's optimism to be at fault. And, to those who shared a nearer intimacy than genial acquaintanceship could offer, is there one left to-day who was disappointed in his Browning or had any deep fault to find with him as a friend ? Surely, no ! He was human to the core, red with the warm blood to the centre of his being ; and if he erred, as he occasionally did — as lately, to the sorrow of all who knew him, he did err — it was the judgment not the instinct that was amiss. He was a poet, after all, and not a philosopher.

It was part of Mr. Browning's large

optimism, of his splendid and self-suffi-
cing physical temperament, that he took
his acquaintances easily — it might almost be said superficially. His poetic
creations crowded out the real world to
a serious extent. With regard to living
men and women he was content to spec-
ulate, but with the children of his brain
the case was different. These were not
the subjects of more or less indolent
conjecture, but of absolute knowledge.
It must be ten years ago, but the im-
pression of the incident is as fresh upon
me as though it happened yesterday,
that Mr. Browning passed from languid
and rather ineffectual discussion of
some persons well known to us both
into vivid and passionate apology for an
act of his own Colombe of Ravenstein.
It was the flash from conventionality to
truth, from talk about people whom he
hardly seemed to see to a record of a
soul that he had formed and could fol-

low through all the mazes of caprice. It was seldom, even in intimacy, I think, that he would talk thus liberally about his sons and daughters of the pen, but that was mainly from a sensible reticence and hatred of common vanity. But when he could be induced to discuss his creations, it was easy to see how vividly the whole throng of them was moving in the hollow of his mind. It is doubtful whether he ever totally forgot any one of the vast assemblage of his characters.

In this close of our troubled century, when to so many of the finest spirits of Europe, in the words of Sully Prud-homme, "Toute la vie ardente et triste Semble anéantie alentour," the robust health of Robert Browning's mind and body has presented a singular and a most encouraging phenomenon. He missed the morbid over-refinement of the age; the processes of his mind were sometimes even a little coarse, and always delightfully direct. For real delicacy he had full appreciation, but he was brutally scornful of all exquisite morbidness. The vibration of his loud voice, his hard fist upon the table, would make very short work with cobwebs. But this external roughness, like the rind of a fruit, merely served to keep the inner sensibilities young and fresh. None of his instincts grew old. Long as he lived, he did not live long enough for one of his ideals to vanish, for one of his enthusiasms to lose its heat; to the last, as he so truly said, he " never doubted clouds would break, Never dreamed, though right were worsted, wrong would triumph." The subtlest of writers, he was the simplest of men, and he learned in serenity what he taught in song.

December 20, 1889.

EPILOGUE

EPILOGUE.

THERE are some verses by Ronsard, which Robert Browning loved, and which I have heard him repeat with enthusiasm. May I quote them here, in the quaint old spelling, and throw them, like a posy of violets, on the marble of his tomb?

> " Que tu es renommée
>   D'estre tombeau nommée
>   D'un de qui l'univers
>   Chante les vers,

> " Et qui oncque en sa vie
>   Ne fut brulé d'envie,
>   Mendiant les honneurs
>   Des grands seigneurs,

> " Ny n'enseigna l'usage
>   De l'amoreux breuvage,

Ny l'art des anciens
Magiciens,

" Mais bien à nos campagnes
Fit voir les Sœurs compagnes
Foulantes l'herbe aux sons
De ses chansons,

" Car il fit a sa lyre
Si bons accords eslire
Qu' il orna de ses chants
Nous et nos champs! "

www.ingramcontent.com/pod-product-compliance
Lightning Source LLC
Chambersburg PA
CBHW060246030726
47493CB00025B/2816